CALGARY PUBLIC LIBRARY
NOVEMBER 2019

P9-EKE-348

For my family – EDL
For Lea and Ábel – JM

Copyright © 2019 Clavis Publishing Inc., New York

Originally published as *Een warme vriendschap* in Belgium and Holland
by Clavis Uitgeverij, Hasselt—Amsterdam, 2018
English translation from the Dutch by Clavis Publishing Inc., New York

Visit us on the Web at www.clavis-publishing.com.

No part of this publication may be reproduced or stored in a retrieval system,
or transmitted in any form or by any means, electronic, mechanical, photocopying,
recording, or otherwise, without the prior written permission of the publisher,
except in the case of brief quotations embodied in critical articles and reviews.
For information regarding permissions, write to Clavis Publishing, info-US@clavisbooks.com.

A Warm Friendship written by Ellen DeLange and illustrated by Jacqueline Molnár

ISBN 978-1-60537-449-9 (hardcover edition)
ISBN 978-1-60537-503-8 (softcover edition)

This book was printed in July 2019 at Nikara, M. R. Štefánika 858/25, 963 01 Krupina, Slovakia.

First Edition
10 9 8 7 6 5 4 3 2 1

Clavis Publishing supports the First Amendment and celebrates the right to read.

A Warm Friendship

Written by Ellen DeLange
Illustrated by Jacqueline Molnár

Clavis

NEW YORK

It's winter. The cold wind blows
big snowflakes through the forest.

Squirrel looks out of her comfortable, warm nest.
She sees something she has never seen before.

There's a snowman.
He is all alone, and is shivering from the cold.
Squirrel quickly jumps from branch to branch
toward him to take a closer look.

"What's wrong?" asks Squirrel.
Snowman looks up and whispers:
"Help me, please . . . I'm *sooo* cold."

Squirrel is startled and quickly scurries away.

Snowman sobs for help, but there's no one else around
who can hear him . . .

Back in her cozy, warm nest,
Squirrel keeps thinking of Snowman,
all alone out there in the cold.

She has to come up with a plan to help him.

Despite the cold, she rushes down the tree
to ask her friends for help.
With a scarf between her teeth,
she runs back to see if Snowman is still there.

And she's not alone!

There are Reindeer and Raccoon,
helping her carry the huge woolen scarf.

Oh, look—there are more animals!

The birds are holding a colorful knitted
blanket with their beaks.
And Hare, Mouse, and Porcupine have scarves too.

Together, they wrap up the shivering snowman.

It doesn't take long to cover Snowman up
with a thick layer of blankets and scarves.
He looks amazing!

"Are you feeling better?" Squirrel asks.
Snowman can smile again.
"Mm, it feels very nice and warm."

From that day on Squirrel and Snowman are best friends.
They have so much fun together that the other animals
come out of the forest to join them.

Everyone hopes that their friendship will last forever . . .

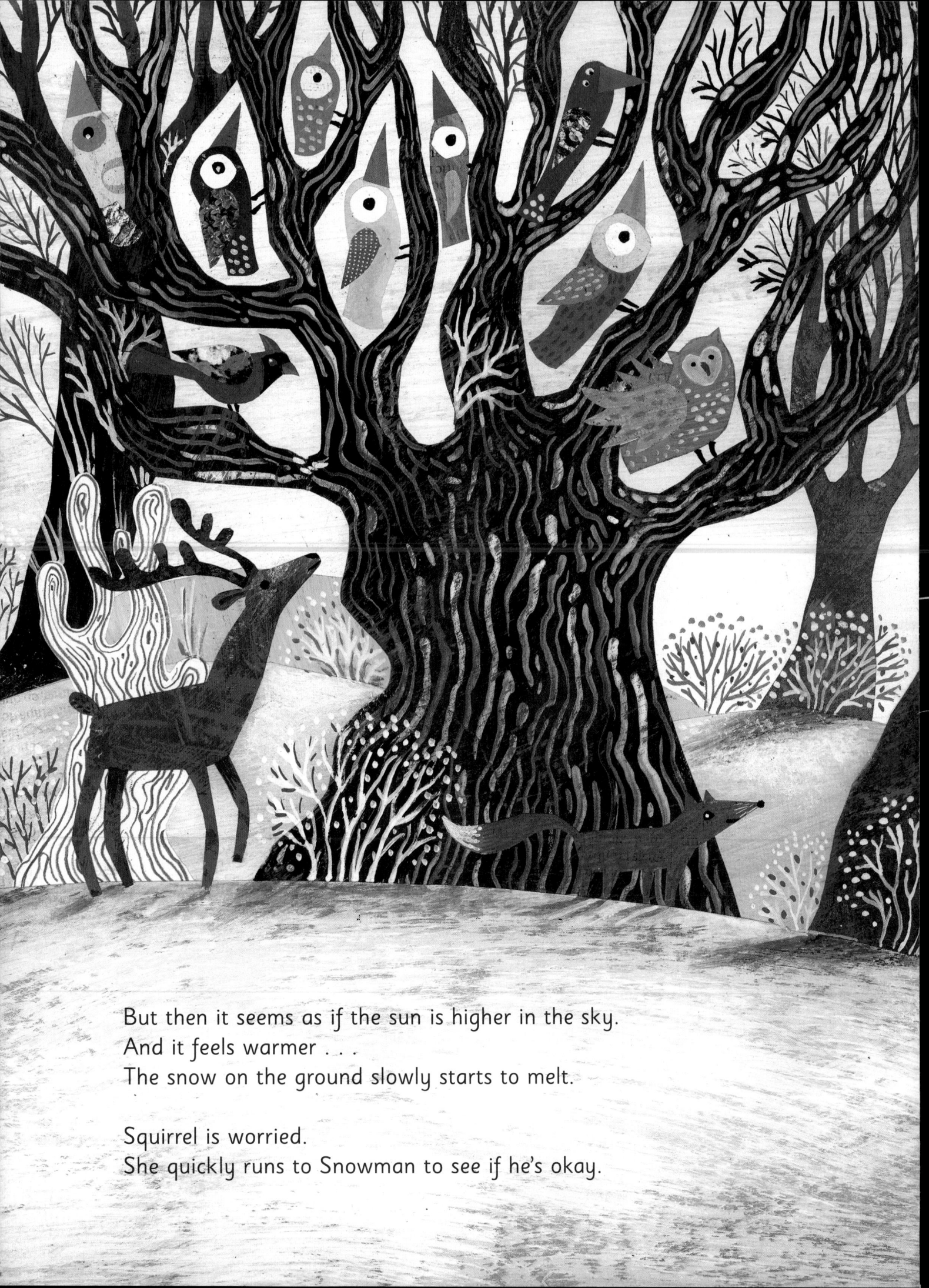

But then it seems as if the sun is higher in the sky.
And it feels warmer . . .
The snow on the ground slowly starts to melt.

Squirrel is worried.
She quickly runs to Snowman to see if he's okay.

Thank goodness! Snowman's still there and he is happier than ever. Squirrel is relieved.

All the forest animals snuggle in tight for a good night's sleep.

Every day, Squirrel's friendship with Snowman
grows stronger and stronger.
She is very happy that they can still play together,
even while it is getting warmer and warmer.

The days fly by . . .

Until one morning, Squirrel finds an empty spot in the forest.
There's now only a pile of blankets and scarves
where Snowman used to be.
He has melted . . .

Squirrel is very sad that her friend is gone.

All the animals from the forest come together.
They carry the blankets and scarves away in silence.
Everybody misses Snowman.

"Don't be sad," says Owl softly, as he puts a scarf around Squirrel's neck.
"Look around and you will see that Snowman is always with you.
In every flower, in every leaf, and especially in all of our hearts."